THE TRAGEDY AT CAMBRIA

Sherrie J. Lyons

ISBN Paperback: 978-1-64873-335-2

First Edition Oregon Literary Review 1, no. 1 (Winter/Spring 2006), www.oregonliteraryreview.org

Media Contact: Writers Publishing House
info@writerspublishinghouse.com

Printed in the United States of America
Published by Writers Publishing House
Prescott, AZ 86301

Cover and Interior Design by
Creative Artistic Excellence

THE TRAGEDY AT CAMBRIA

THE TRAGEDY AT CAMBRIA

DRAMATIS PERSONAE

John, King of Cambria
Beatrice, Queen of Cambria
Scott, Prince of Cambria *& heir to the throne*
Janette, *Prince Scott's inamorata*
Prosecutor
Soothsayer
Herald

Jailer (Orth)
Attendant 1
Kingsman
Princess Winnicott
Princess Hunnicutt
Princess Mary Grace
Midwife

Non- or collectively speaking: Lords, Ladies, Citizens of Cambria, Attendant 2, Trumpeters, Guards, Princess Pennyweight, Unnamed Princesses 1, 2, 3, Jailer's wife and family, Unnamed Babies 1, 2

*   *   *

PROLOGUE

Enter SOOTHSAYER, *solus.*

SOOTH.

Behold a land where ancient statutes rule,

Where laws that once served well have since waxed cruel,

Where lovers are confined to marriage bed,

And babies got by those who are unwed

Are oftentimes forsaken—or born dead.

What good can come from such a place as this?

Where citizens can see what is amiss

But turn their heads pretending all is well?

A child, a bastard child, I do foretell—

But not before our king knows royal hell.   *10*

[*Exit.*

ACT I

SCENE 1

Castle Great Hall; TRUMPETERS, HERALD, *and* GUARDS *standing;*
PROSECUTOR, JANETTE, LORDS, LADIES, *and* CITIZENS *seated.*

[*Trumpet flourish.*]

HERALD

All rise and pay due homage to King John.

[GALLERY *stands.*]

Enter KING; *stands in front of his throne, facing the gallery.*

GALLERY

Hail to John, our just and able sovereign!

Enter QUEEN *and* PRINCE.

HERALD

[*Surprised*]

. . . And pay due homage to our queen and prince.

GALLERY

Hail to the queen! Hail to the royal prince!

KING

We thank you fellow citizens. Please sit.

[*All but* PROSECUTOR, HERALDS, GUARDS, *and* ROYALTY *sit.*]

1

KING

[*Aside to* QUEEN]

What brings you to this common trial this day?

You commonly beg leave to stay away.

QUEEN

[*Aside to* KING]

Our son, the prince, has vested interest here.

KING

[*Aside to* QUEEN]

Too true; someday, he'll have this work, my dear.

I grant him sit and keep attentive ear.   *10*

[ROYALTY *sits, with* QUEEN *on King's left and* PRINCE *on King's right.*]

KING

High prosecutor, call the first accused.

PROSECUTOR

Guard, bring the prisoner forth.

KING

                                                            What joke is this?

We're not amused. Young maiden, please step fore.

PROSECUTOR

She is no maiden, Majesty, but whore.

The child within her womb's the evidence.

2

KING

Accused, what are you called?

JANETTE

"Whore," Majesty.

KING

Ha! State your name before this court of law.

JANETTE

My name's Janette, though few men know it.

PROSECUTOR

[*Aside*]

More men have likely known her than her name.

JANETTE

I go by Jane, plain Jane, Your Majesty.   *20*

PROSECUTOR

Plainly, she is anything but plain, Sire.

Her beauty likely lured men twixt her thighs;

Her sensual smile encouraged deep desire,

Abetted by the sparkle in her eyes.

JANETTE

Upon my word, I am an orphan, Sire.

My mother died when I was but age ten.

I eke a living selling wood for fire.

My liege, I do not fraternize with men.

3

PROSECUTOR

Aye, Jane's an orphan, that I grant is true:

Her sire, a thief, passed on when she was two; *30*

He swung from prison gallows, I recall;

His head was cleaned by birds out on the wall.

Jane's saintly mum lies cold from sailors' pox,

Acquired from working ships down at the docks.

But ere she died, she taught Jane all she knew—

And that is why Jane's standing here 'fore you.

JANETTE

My mother did not die of pox, I swear.

'Twas plague that took her from this earthly place.

She nursed sick swabs when no one else would dare.

I learned compassion, mercy—not disgrace. *40*

KING

And yet you do appear to be disgraced.

JANETTE

If finding love and happiness is wrong,

What reason has God put us on this land?

KING

To test us, Jane—He wants us to be strong

Ere we sit down in heaven by his hand.

Unwedded weakness of the flesh *is* wrong:

It violates our savior's Holy Plan;

Nor does a baby born from sin belong

On land, beside a righteous Cambrian—

Or by our Lord—such mocks His Prime Command. *50*

KING (Continued)

The prosecutor claims you are with child.

Do you deny the charge that he has brought?

Speak truthfully if you have been defiled,

For time will tell the truth, if you do not.

JANETTE

I won't confess that I have been "defiled"—

I loved a man and got his bastard child.

I love him still and love his child within.

I don't believe God thinks our love's a sin!

[GALLERY *gasps.*]

PROSECUTOR

My lord, this girl has clearly lost her case,

[*Aside*]

If not her mind.

[*To All*]

Her stance is a disgrace   *60*

To all who know and heed the word of God.

She's testified that she's an infidel!

For that alone she's bound to go to hell.

Make judgment now and sentence her, Your Grace.

PRINCE

Let not her words be taken for her thoughts!

Her shame and anger likely shade her speech;

Plus she is young—and under-schooled—and odd.

Discount her outburst, Father, I beseech.

5

KING

My son, I see that I have raised you well:

You look beyond and mark what others miss, 70

But it is not your place to speak in court.

Sit silently, like good Queen Beatrice.

QUEEN

My husband, I would have a word with you.

[*Aside to* KING]

What you have said is absolutely true,

But I propose a trial of something new:

Within a fortnight, Scott turns seventeen—

The age that you first sat upon this chair.

You said yourself one day he'd have this job;

Let's test how he would judge this girl's affair.

KING

[*Aside to* QUEEN]

The case is simple, that is simply true. 80

As such, a simpleton could follow through

Our maze of law and know what he must do . . .

QUEEN

[*Aside to* KING]

Then it's decided, Scott will judge this case.

KING

[*Aside to* QUEEN]

. . . And yet, my public may not like the change.

Our laws do not allow me to replace

Myself for son, until he is of age.

KING (Continued)

And what of Jane, whom I will have to face,

If she cries foul when told of the exchange?

QUEEN

[*Aside to* KING]

But you're the *king*. What matters what they say?

What *you* say goes. It's always been that way.   *90*

KING

[*Aside to* QUEEN]

What I say goes because it is the law,

And law applies to all, including me.

I can't allow our son to judge Jane's case—

But I shall have him choose her penalty.

[*To* GALLERY]

Good citizens, our prince soon comes of age.

Until that time, he cannot judge a cause,

But I shall have him choose Jane's penalty,

(Assuming she's convicted by our laws).

JANETTE

My liege, I do not wish Prince Scott to choose!

PRINCE

Nor do I wish the honor of that deed!   *100*

KING

My mind is set; my son, you can't refuse.

[*To* JANETTE]

And you've no say;

KING (Continued)

[*To* ALL]

It's done, so we'll proceed:

[*To* JANETTE]

The prosecutor's right, you've lost your suit—
The proof outweighs whatever you believe.
But all's not lost if you inform us of
The father's name—we'll grant a full reprieve.

JANETTE

And what will happen to the man I name?

KING

He'll marry you and lift your veil of shame.
And that will save both you and child from hell—
Just name the man, and all will turn out well.   *110*

JANETTE

But what will happen if he cannot wed?

KING

You mean he's bound by vows, yet shared his bed?

[GALLERY *gasps.*]

KING

Then he, not you nor child, will pay the price
Of sin. He'll make a manly sacrifice:
Castration is our cure for straying men.
It guarantees a rogue won't roam again.

JANETTE

And guarantees he'll father no more heirs.

KING

Aye, that's the consequence for rash affairs.

Jane, name the man, and all will turn out well.

JANETTE

I won't, my liege. I'll never, ever tell!   *120*

KING

Then we declare you guilty of the crime

Of "whoring with resultant fetal tot."

We thank the prosecutor for his time,

And now we'll hear your sentence from Prince Scott.

[PROSECUTOR *sits.*]

PRINCE

I know the law in such a case as this

Requires I choose Janette or babe to die.

We can't allow both whore and child to live:

They'll drain our wealth and pain our God on high.

[*To* JANETTE]

Janette, you do not seem to understand

That both can live if you'll just name the man.   *130*

You need more time to contemplate your fate—

[*Aside*]

And I need time to formulate a plan.

[*To* GUARD]

Guard, take Jane to a cell to ruminate.

[GALLERY *grumbles.*]

[*Exeunt* GUARD *and* JANETTE.

                    KING

        High prosecutor, call the next accused.

[PROSECUTOR *stands.*]

                    PROSECUTOR

    There are no more.

                    KING

            Then everyone's excused.   *135*

[*Curtain drops.*

                    SCENE 2

Prison; JAILER *standing;* JANETTE *in cell.*

Enter PRINCE.

                    JAILER

    Good morrow, good Prince Scott.

                    PRINCE

                Good morrow, sirrah.

    I'm here to see the prisoner called Jane.

JAILER

She's not permitted visitors, my lord.

Alas, your morning's ride has been in vain,

For none can visit by the king's decree.

PRINCE

My father's writ does not apply to me.

You will allow me entrance through the gate,

Since I'm the one who's master of Jane's fate.

JAILER

I fear I will be victim of his ire,

If I don't serve the will of our good sire.   *10*

PRINCE

Fear not, and trust I know my father well;

But if he's mad, I'll tell him 'twas my fault:

I ordered you to take me to Jane's cell—

Insisted when you said that I must halt.

And here's a token of my thanks for you.

[PRINCE *gives bribe.*]

PRINCE

Now open up and let your prince pass through.

JAILER

All right, I'll let you enter through the gate,

But prince or not, I have to search you first.

I'm sure that you'd expect to do the same,

If by odd fate our places were reversed.   *20*

[JAILER *lets* PRINCE *in and begins frisking him.*]

PRINCE

I can't believe you think I'd bring birth herbs
Or beans to help Jane end her pregnancy.
You think I want the whore to lose the child
By sipping silphium mixed in her tea?

JAILER

Too often I've seen trulls escape their fates:
They're freed from death aft' visits by their "aunts."
The "proof" is lost within their dirty sheets—
My lord, turn round, and let me grope your pants.

PRINCE

Enough, you've done your duty far too well!

JAILER

Well, good enough—come, trail me to her cell.   *30*

JANETTE

My prince!

PRINCE

[*To* JAILER]

Allow me time alone with Jane.

JAILER

My lord, I think it best if I remain.

12

PRINCE

Then think again. Now lock me in with her.

JAILER

Since you insist, I'll do your bidding, sir.

[*Exit* JAILER.

[PRINCE *and* JANETTE *embrace.*]

PRINCE

My love, I thought that he would never leave.

JANETTE

My love, I thought that you would never come.

PRINCE

[*Aside*]

Had I not come inside!

[*To* JANETTE]

How fare you, Jane?

JANETTE

I'm fair enough. I truly can't complain.

PRINCE

I'm glad to hear your words. I've worried so—

JANETTE

[*In tears*]

The cell is dim; the nights are cold as snow;   40

JANETTE (Continued)

The food tastes foul; one guard plays Romeo—

But all is fair; I truly can't complain—

I got my due for loving you, my swain.

PRINCE

I'm sorry, Jane. It's all so inhumane.

What kind of law requires the death of she

Who bears a child without first properly

Obtaining grace through the formality

Of unity 'fore God? Or otherwise,

The death of spawn the dawn of its first day?

JANETTE

Yet that's our way.

PRINCE

               The law is clearly flawed . . .   *50*

I cannot bear to sentence you to death,

Nor can I bear to drown our unborn tot.

JANETTE

I cannot bear to bear this child for naught.

Choose me, my prince; choose me, I beg you Scott!

PRINCE

I'd sooner 'fess my sin and pay the price.

JANETTE

No, Scott, you mustn't make that sacrifice!

Someday, you'll find a princess you can wed,

JANETTE (Continued)

And when you do, you'll do your part in bed
And get her with the seed of royal blood
To show the world that you're a virile stud. *60*
That means you must conceal your love for me.

PRINCE

I would that you were born to royalty—
I'll never love another such as you.
My love is constant, endless, pure, and true.

JANETTE

And so is mine. Whatever shall we do?

PRINCE

I thought that you might lie and name a man,
A lowly, lewd, and drunken thief or such,
Declare that he had forced himself on you
And pricked you with depraved, unwanted touch.

JANETTE

How dare you call a thief a lowly drunk! *70*
Have you forgotten he who was my sire?
You'd let them geld a needy innocent?
You'd ask me to become a sinful liar?

PRINCE

Of course not, Jane! 'Twas just a fleeting thought—
My desperation drove me to wild schemes.
Besides, you've spoiled all hope for that defense—
"I love him still," you claimed, or so meseems.

PRINCE (Continued)

[*Aside*]

A damning phrase, though laced with innocence.

Oh wicked, vile, unholy consequence.

[*To* JANETTE]

But do not worry—I've another plan.   *80*

My mother knows what you and I have done.

She tried to intercede before for us,

And now she'll close the venture she's begun:

She'll have a conversation with our king,

And criticize the harshness of our laws.

She'll make him see our judgments are unjust;

She'll gently sway him over to our cause.

He'll sympathize and end our dreadful plight.

I swear to you, our king will make things right.

JANETTE

I would I could believe your soothing words.   *90*

PRINCE

You can. My father loves me more than life;

Thus, he would do near anything for me.

He'll grant me liberty to choose my wife.

JANETTE

You can't believe he'll let you choose Plain Jane!

A commoner? A heretic? A whore?

Scott, you will rule his realm when he's passed on.

He loves you lots—but loves his kingdom more!

PRINCE

Then I will trick him into letting me

Select the woman whom I want to wed.

I'll do it Friday at my birthday fête.   *100*

JANETTE

I trust you will, yet feel a sense of dread.

PRINCE

The chill you feel is nothing more than wind.

It's seeping twixt these gloomy walls of stone.

I'll tell the guard to see you get a quilt.

For now, I'll warm your body with my own.

[*They embrace and kiss.*]

JANETTE

Let's lie upon this mat they call a bed

And close our eyes to all our miseries,

Then clasp each other one more time with fire

And burn our love into our memories.

PRINCE

Alas, here comes an ill-timed chaperone.   *110*

Jane, mark my words, for soon I must depart:

When you feel glum, please know you're not alone—

I hold your image firmly in my heart.

I promise I will fix this awful mess.

I will not let you nor our baby die.

Anon we all will live in happiness.

Don't cry, my love. My spirit's always nigh.

17

JANETTE

I thank you for your call and for your words

And truly think you love me with your life,

But I confide that you have wounded me: *120*

I feel as though you've slit me with your knife.

Scott, clarify one thing before you go:

You said in court you think that I am odd . . .

I have to know the truth, so is it so?

PRINCE

Yes, Jane, I swear it now before our God.

I could not love a common commoner.

But you're unique, a rainbow in my life—

A rare and precious oddity, for sure;

That's why I want to take you for my wife.

[*They embrace.*]

JANETTE

I've been a fool and don't deserve you, Prince,   *130*

But now at least I have the confidence

To sleep at night and know you're here with me

In heart and soul, if not near physically.

Go now, my love, and worry not of Jane,

For all is well. I truly can't complain.

Re-enter JAILER.

PRINCE

Good sirrah, you may let me out of here.

My business with the girl is now complete.

[JAILER *releases* PRINCE. *They walk away.*]

PRINCE

I charge you to bring Jane a coverlet;

She's cold at night with just one threadbare sheet.

JAILER

If she'd decided to cooperate,   *140*

She would have been warm several nights ago.

PRINCE

Explain your meaning of *cooperate.*

JAILER

I mean forsake the one she calls her beau.

She needs incentive to betray the lout.

Until she squawks, she ought to go without.

PRINCE

A detainee deserves a clean warm quilt

Regardless of his innocence or guilt,

So see that everyone who's held in here

Sleeps well this night. Are my instructions clear?

JAILER

Indeed, my lord. I'll do as you command.   *150*

PRINCE

Though truthfully, you do not understand?

It's not our job to punish people here.

We're holding them until their souls meet God.

19

PRINCE (Continued)

It's He—not you nor I—that they should fear.

JAILER

My lord, I'm loath to treat the scum like guests.

PRINCE

Then fake respect—but honor my behests.   *156*

[*Exit* PRINCE.

SCENE 3

King's chamber; KING *disrobing;* ATTENDANTS 1 & 2.

[*Knock.*]

KING

Go see who seeks admittance to my ear.

[ATTENDANT 1 *answers knock.*]

ATTENDANT 1

Your Majesty, Queen Beatrice is here.

KING

You are dismissed.

[*Exeunt* ATTENDANTS.

KING

Come in, my treasured dear!

Enter QUEEN.

KING

What brings you to my chamber on this night?

QUEEN

I thought you might desire to hold me near.

KING

I always do, and we can do the deed,

But I suspect your motives aren't sincere.

I think that you want something else from me,

And I'd be pleased to listen to your plea,

So tell me what's been troubling you this week.   *10*

We'll make a plan to fix it at first light.

Then we can concentrate on pleasuring

Without undue distractions through the night.

QUEEN

I must admit my situation's odd:

The soothsayer approached me last day noon.

She said that I must come to you this night

And join with you beneath the brimming moon.

KING

Indeed! I'll have to have a talk with her

And thank her for her wise advice with coins.

KING (Continued)

I should have thought to do this years ago

To still the ceaseless stirring in my loins.

20

QUEEN

"Indeed," *indeed!* You've never once complained.

KING

I spoke in jest! The witch is addle-brained.

We don't need her to rally us to breed.

You know you satisfy my every need.

Ignore the bat. She "sees" what isn't there.

Place faith in God—He sees what's everywhere.

QUEEN

You're right, and yet she has a certain skill

For knowing things that I have shared with none;

For instance, Scott weighs heavy on my heart,

And she discerned my problem is our son.

30

KING

Then she advised that you should mate with me,

And that would ease the burden on your heart?

My love cures all—I'm quite the remedy!

For you, my queen, I'll gladly do my part!

QUEEN

You've made your point: I sound ridiculous.

But when she spoke, the seer sounded sure:

A mist of darkness shrouds your monarchy.

What harm is there in trying out her cure?

KING

The harm is that it bolsters sorcery,   *40*

A doctrine that I'd like to see disproved—

But I will lie beneath the moon with you,

Because it's been a while, and I'm so moved.

You say the seer snagged you yesterday,

But I detected moodiness all week.

Please tell me what is wrong regarding Scott.

I cannot help, if you nor he won't speak.

QUEEN

In just one day our son turns seventeen.

By law, he then becomes a full-fledged man.

He wants to make a difference in the world—   *50*

He wants to make it better if he can.

We've raised a warm and tenderhearted son.

He's honest, kind, and fair to everyone.

KING

Is he afraid he'll be perceived as weak?

QUEEN

Perhaps by you; but hold, and let me speak:

Recall the trial for which he must choose tween

A newborn child or girl who's just sixteen.

He knows the law and wants to do his job;

He wants to show the world that he's a man,

But his young heart is filled with sympathy,   *60*

So he's developing a brazen plan.

Our son believes our laws are harsh and wrong—

That death is too definitive a fix.

23

QUEEN (Continued)

He wants to bring the matter 'fore all folks.

He wants to change our country's politics.

He thinks that banishment should be a choice

Of he who has to make the legal call.

He wants to see the change passed right away.

He's going to give this hopeless plan his all.

I cannot tell him that his plan won't pass,   *70*

Although I know it in my breaking heart,

And if he fails at this, his first attempt

At winning ballots, it may be the start

Of lack of confidence in him—by self

And by the people he will one day rule.

And John, our son's in love with love, I fear.

Oh, how I wish that he were still in school!

For he's the one with stirring in his loins.

He says he wants to wed within the year!

He says he wants to choose a wife himself!   *80*

He says he will not let us interfere!

KING

Good Lord! Can you have any more to say?

QUEEN

Forgive me, John. My tongue near ran away.

KING

Now I can see that which the seer saw:

When you're distraught, it's always due to Scott.

But Scott's attempts to boldly blaze a trail

Do not portend a darkness on our reign.

KING (Continued)

His independence shows we've raised him well.

The only problem is that girl called Jane.

So I will make the choice for young Prince Scott,   *90*

But he will voice the outcome as his own.

We three will know that I'm the one who chose;

To other folks, the truth will be unknown.

And once Jane's fate has been declared by Scott,

He will not have the need to change our laws.

QUEEN

But he may try to do so anyway.

He's adamant that they contain vile flaws.

KING

You're right that Scott might lose his following,

If he pursues his well-intentioned goal,

For throngs will think he's rash and uninformed,   *100*

Instead of feeling that he's in control.

Our citizens aren't prone to pass Scott's plan

Because they know our constitution states

That we will never cast our criminals out

To let them gather at another's gates.

It isn't right to send our friends our scum,

Plus we would have to take *their* vermin in.

Our older subjects understand our stance;

They'd never cast the votes Scott needs to win.

The constitution's rightly hard to change   *110*

Because it is the highest of our laws,

But I'm empowered to write my own decrees

And thus have means to change what Scott calls "flaws."

KING (Continued)

Tomorrow I will write a special writ

That places convict-trades upon our books,

And that will give a king another choice

In sentencing our thugs and whores and crooks.

The writ should squelch Scott's need for banishment,

For if a country's fain to take our scum

By ones or more in interchange for theirs,   *120*

We'll have a law in place to send them some.

QUEEN

And of our son's request to seek a spouse?

KING

He's old enough to know what that will mean.

If he insists he's ripe to play at house,

It's not our place to try to intervene.

Tomorrow night we host a gay affair

To celebrate as Scott turns seventeen,

And for a gift I'll let him choose his wife,

If he's determined he must get his queen.

He'll have to wait at least six months to wed   *130*

To give you time to make grand wedding plans,

And that will give us time to get to know

And sell his choice to all the Cambrians.

QUEEN

You are so wise and loving, my good king.

In truth, I thought our talk would not go well.

I feared that you'd be angry with our son

And fight against his efforts to rebel.

KING

I well remember being seventeen,

For that's the year I turned my mother grey!

I don't want Scott to do the same to you. *140*

QUEEN

Too late, I fear, but thank you anyway!

KING

Do you agree our business is now done?

QUEEN

I do, my lord. I know of nothing more.

KING

Then I submit, it's time to have some fun.

Let's take a stroll along the moonlit shore,

And find a place with decent coverture

To shed our garb and test the seer's cure. *147*

[*Exeunt.*

ACT II
SCENE 1

Prison; JAILER *standing;* JANETTE *in cell.*

Enter PRINCE.

JAILER

Good day and joyous birthday, good Prince Scott!

PRINCE

Indeed, this day is good, and I am psyched!
So open up and lead me to Janette!

[PRINCE *offers bribe.*]

JAILER

My lord, I can't. Our righteous sire disliked
That I allowed you contact with her once.
He said his writ applied to everyone—
Specifically, his adolescent son.
He made me swear I would not let you in.
If he finds out I broke my word to him,
He'll have my head or hang me for my sin.   *10*
He said you'd chosen which of them would die,
And thus you need not speak again with her.
And then he took the quilts from all the cons
And docked me two weeks' pay—I'm blotted, sir.

PRINCE

By God, I'll pay the money back to you!

28

PRINCE (Continued)

I hope you told him all the fault was mine.

JAILER

If I'd done that, he would have fired me, sir.

I think I got off easy with the fine.

PRINCE

Perhaps you're right. I should have asked him first,

Ere coming here or changing his set rule.   *20*

But don't despair—I'll see your blot reversed.

You'll not be wrongly tagged for ridicule.

JAILER

I thank you, sir. I knew you'd do me right.

PRINCE

I'll snag the king and talk with him this day,

And on my oath, I'll champion your plight.

I'll see that you receive your two weeks' pay,

And have your record cleared before this night.

JAILER

Again, I thank you, sir, for your good deed.

PRINCE

Before I go, there's still one thing I need.

[PRINCE *offers bigger bribe.*]

JAILER

I cannot let you in the jail, Prince Scott.

PRINCE

You think that's what I need, but it is not:

I only need to *speak* to the girl, Jane.

I promised I would visit her this day.

If I don't come, she'll label me a rake.

You understand, my honor is at stake.

JAILER

You're asking me to bring the whore out here?

PRINCE

What harm is there? You know she can't escape.

JAILER

I cannot risk the loss of my career!

PRINCE

I'll help you out, if you get in a scrape.

JAILER

I have a wife and kids whom I hold dear!

PRINCE

I understand, but you have naught to fear:

I know the king is two hours' ride from here.

[PRINCE *offers bigger bribe.*]

JAILER

[Aside]

I have four kids, and Mum is moving in.

I'll let God weigh the poundage of my sin.

[To PRINCE]

All right, I'll bring the whore out here for you,

But you must keep your conversation short.

Just tell the girl you kept your word to her,

Then let her know you'll deal with her at court.

[*Exit* JAILER.

PRINCE

This day I am a man—or so I'm told—

But why the sun has license to so rule,   *50*

I've never thought to think about before . . .

I'll bet it was adjudged by some damn fool!

I look no older than I did last month.

I feel no older than I did last night.

Was I a man a day or moon ago?

Am I still yet a boy in God's clear sight?

The supposition that I'm now a man

Holds much import to everyone I see.

They seem to think I'm somehow rare and grand;

But they would cringe to know the real me.   *60*

It makes no matter if I'm boy or man—

I do not like my person either way.

Unlike fine wine, I've not improved with age—

I'm still the sinning wretch of yesterday.

But lo, the sun's still rising in the sky.

By this day's end, I swear I'll change my ways!

31

PRINCE (Continued)

I'll be a man in God's and my own eyes!

I'll be deserving of my people's praise!

Re-enter JAILER *with* JANETTE.

PRINCE

[*To* JAILER]

Go stand by yonder tree while we converse.

[*Exit* JAILER.

PRINCE

How fare you, Jane?

JANETTE

I've gone from fair to worse.   *70*

PRINCE

I'm sorry, love. I heard about the quilt.

But I bear news that's sure to warm you through:

The queen has spoken to our king for me,

And she has done what I forespake she'd do!

She used her wiles to make him see my way—

This night, he plans to let me choose my wife!

He also penned a special writ this day,

A writ that I could use to save your life!

But I won't have to use the special writ,

Because this night I'll choose to marry you.   *80*

Our sins will come to light, but once we're wed,

The citizens will know our love is true,

32

PRINCE (Continued)

And they will overlook the wrongs we've done.

And if they don't—so what?—our trial is through.

I wish that you were free to stand near me

And hold my hand as I declare we'll wed,

But at first light I'll ride to fetch you home.

Tomorrow night, I'll warm you in my bed!

[*Trumpet flourish.*]

Re-enter JAILER *on the run.*

JAILER

My God, our king is coming here again!

PRINCE

[*To* JANETTE]

Farewell, my love, until tomorrow morn.   *90*

JANETTE

[*To* PRINCE]

But I've so much I need to say to you!

JAILER

My lord, did you not hear your father's horn?

Away with you!

[*Exit* PRINCE.

JAILER

Come whore, you must return!

Enter KING *with* KINGSMAN *and* ENTOURAGE.

KING

Arrest that man! And take Jane to her cell!

KINGSMAN

A man escapes!

KING

He's not of our concern.

JAILER

Forgive me, Sire. I—

KING

You will have a turn

To speak at court next week.

[KINGSMAN *with* JAILER *and* JANETTE *enter prison.*]

KING

We must ride on:

The princesses inside our coach need rest.

This night they'll want to look their very best.

[*Exeunt* KING *and* ENTOURAGE.

JANETTE

[*In cell*]

I love you more than life itself, Prince Scott,   *100*

And I believe that you believe your words,

34

JANETTE (Continued)

But I'm afraid your plan is like a pot

That's dropped and breaks into a hundred sherds.

No matter how you try to fix the pot,

You cannot realign its garnitures,

And I'm afraid your sire, our Sire, is not

Aligned to the same plan as mine and yours.

He came to me and spoke between the bars.

He said that you'd decided I should live—

Our child will drown, and I must bear the scars.   *110*

He said to pray and ask God to forgive

My sins, when he's the one who ought to pray.

Imagine killing one's own relative!

And since I can't, I've planned my own escape.

Forgive me, Scott: If I can't be your wife,

I'm going to leave our child for you to shape—

I have no choice but that to take my life.

My love, I pray your party plan works through,

But if it fails, I'll do what I must do.   *119*

SCENE 2

King's chamber; KING *dressing;* ATTENDANTS 1 & 2.

[*Knock.*]

KING

Go see who seeks admittance to my ear.

[ATTENDANT 1 *answers knock.*]

35

ATTENDANT 1

Your Majesty, the royal prince is here.

KING

[*To* ATTENDANT 2]

Unloose my shirt. I need a larger size.

[*To* PRINCE]

Come in, dear son, and let us see your guise.

Enter PRINCE.

[PRINCE *models.*]

ATTENDANT 1

My Lord! He looks so grand and smart and wise!

KING

[*To* PRINCE]

Your suit suits you, but that is no surprise:

You look a man, because you are this night.

I'm sure our guests will marvel at your sight.

[ATTENDANTS *dress* KING *in larger shirt.*]

PRINCE

I thank you, Sire, but I don't feel quite right.

KING

[*To* ATTENDANTS]

This shirt fits fine. Begone until first light.

10

[*Exeunt* ATTENDANTS.

KING

It's normal, son, to feel a bit uptight

When up on stage—but you'll get passed the fright.

Relax, imbibe, enjoy your special night.

PRINCE

The spotlight's not what's turned my face to white.

I've made mistakes and need to set things right.

KING

To keep our guests on hold is impolite.

[PRINCE *doesn't move.*]

[KING *sighs.*]

KING

I know no one who's perfect in God's sight.

He'll pardon you, because you are contrite.

PRINCE

But that won't change the outcome of my lies.

KING

Indeed it will—at least in God's clear eyes!   *20*

PRINCE

But Father, what if someone blameless dies?

KING

Scott, stop! You've no need to hyperbolize.

[*Knock.*]

[KING *opens door.*]

Enter QUEEN.

QUEEN

What's keeping you? You know our guests are here!

KING

Our son is just a tad bit nervous, dear.   *24*

[*Exeunt.*

SCENE 3

Castle ballroom; KING, QUEEN, *and* PRINCE; GUESTS: LORDS, LADIES,
ROYALTY, *and* CITIZENS *dancing and milling;* TRUMPETERS *and* HERALD
standing at posts.

[*Dance ends. Trumpet flourish.*]

HERALD

Attention everyone! The time has come
To give Prince Scott his gift.

KING

Come hither, son.

[PRINCE *joins* KING.]

KING

We're gathered here because Scott's now a man.

We're pleased to see the way that he has grown.

In fact, we hear that Scott has hatched a plan;

We're proud that he has viewpoints of his own.

The mumblings that have made their way to us

Involve the rumblings of his youthful loins:

We hear he wants to marry right away.

We hear he wants to *choose* whom he adjoins.   *10*

[CITIZENS *gasp.*]

We thought to give Scott jewels or an estate—

Perhaps a herd of best-bred royal mounts—

[CITIZENS *ooh.*]

But he's not one to covet earthly things:

To him, the thought behind the gift's what counts.

[CITIZENS *aah.*]

And so we've thought to give him what he wants

And let him choose the woman he will wed—

PRINCE

I thank you, Sire, for granting my desire!

It means so much to have your go-ahead!

39

KING

You're welcome, Son. We're glad to hear your cheer.

We're sure that you'll be pleased with what we've done—   *20*

PRINCE

And so I am! I'll tell you whom I want!

KING

Show patience, Scott. We've helped you with your hunt:

We've plucked the world's most fitting princesses

And gathered them inside our palace gates,

And now we'll bring them forth for you to meet.

It's time to introduce the candidates!

PRINCE

[*To* KING]

Dear lord! My sire, you do not understand—

[*Trumpet flourish.*]

KING

Consider each one carefully, Prince Scott.

HERALD

Presenting royal Princess Winnicott!

Enter PRINCESS WINNICOTT.

KING

[*To* PRINCE]

Behold her youth—and she owns beaucoup land!   *30*

KING (Continued)

When she approaches, bow and kiss her hand.

PRINCE

[*Aside*]

Her youth? She sucked a wet nurse yesterday!

She looks like she is all of ten years old!

[*To* WINNICOTT]

Good evening, Princess. Welcome to my fête.

WINNICOTT

Good evening, Prince. If I may be so bold,

Choose me above my sib—she's fat and old.

[WINNICOTT *moves into crowd.*]

[*Trumpet flourish.*]

HERALD

Presenting royal Princess Hunnicutt!

Enter PRINCESS HUNNICUTT.

KING

[*To* PRINCE]

Behold her glow—her cheeks look ripe, like fruit.

PRINCE

[*Aside*]

Admittedly, her face is rather cute,

But paint and gown can't hide a pumpkin gut

PRINCE (Continued)

Or over-ripened cheeks of melon butt.

[*To* HUNNICUTT]

Good evening, Princess. Welcome to my fête.

HUNNICUTT

Good evening, Prince. If I may be so bold,

Choose me above my sib—she's spoiled and cold.

[HUNNICUTT *moves into crowd.*]

[*Trumpet flourish.*]

HERALD

Presenting royal Princess Mary Grace!

Enter PRINCESS MARY GRACE.

KING

[*To* PRINCE]

Behold her stately carriage and her poise.

PRINCE

[*Aside*]

Again, I cannot criticize her face,

But she is known to favor girls o'er boys.

[*To* MARY GRACE]

Good evening, Princess. Welcome to my fête.

MARY GRACE

Good evening, Prince. If I may be so bold,

50

MARY GRACE (Continued)

My dowry's chest is filled with purest gold.

[MARY GRACE *moves into crowd.*]

PRINCE

[*Aside*]

Your father wants to prove that you are straight,

But I won't buy you—nor your father's bait.

[*Trumpet flourish.*]

HERALD

Presenting royal Princess Pennyweight!

Enter PRINCESS PENNYWEIGHT.

PRINCE

[*Aside*]

The only maid whose foot fits in the glass

Is waiting anxiously for me to ride—

[*To* PENNYWEIGHT]

Good evening, Princess. Welcome to my fête.

[PENNYWEIGHT *moves into crowd.*]

PRINCE

[*Aside*]

And rescue her from rags and filth and fate,

And honor her by making her my bride.

43

[*Trumpet flourish.*]

Enter UNNAMED PRINCESS 1.

PRINCE

[*Aside*]

I cannot risk embarrassing my sire;   *60*

I know he thought this gift was something grand—

[*To* UNNAMED PRINCESS 1]

Good evening, Princess. Welcome to my fête.

[UNNAMED PRINCESS 1 *moves into crowd.*]

PRINCE

[*Aside*]

But I have *got* to make him understand

That Jane's the one I've chosen for my mate.

[*Trumpet flourish.*]

Enter UNNAMED PRINCESS 2.

PRINCE

[*Aside*]

I must confront him ere this night is o'er

And speak of Jane and also that poor guard.

[*To* UNNAMED PRINCESS 2]

Good evening, Princess. Welcome to my fête.

[UNNAMED PRINCESS 2 *moves into crowd.*]

44

PRINCE

[*Aside*]

I pray to God that he won't take it hard,

But if he does, I can't capitulate.

[*Trumpet flourish.*]

Enter UNNAMED PRINCESS 3.

PRINCE

[*Aside*]

And so I'll smile and show the maids my charm;   *70*

I'll schmooze with them and offer them my arm;

[*To* UNNAMED PRINCESS 3]

Good evening, Princess. Welcome to my fête.

[UNNAMED PRINCESS 3 *moves into crowd.*]

PRINCE

[*Aside*]

I'll twirl with them, and when the clock chimes late,

I'll say goodnight, goodbye—then celebrate

That they are gone, and find my sire alone

Somewhere where I can speak to him of love

[*Trumpet flourish.*]

HERALD

Attention everyone! The time has come

PRINCE

[*Aside*]

That's born of flawless vision from above:

The dragon's breath that's burning in my heart—

The fervent fire that flames my deep desire—   *80*

The searing pain from being kept apart.

No longer can I keep my heat inside!

HERALD

For Scott to name the maid to grace his side.

PRINCE

The world must know that Jane will be my bride!

[GUESTS *gasp.*]

KING

. . . Our friends, I need apologize for Scott.

By moons, he is a man; by booze, he's not.

[GUESTS *laugh.*]

KING

He's dwelled upon the case he has in court,

Then drunk too much and muddled up his speech.

We're pleased he takes Jane's sentence earnestly

And pleased he's chosen *Hunnicutt*, a peach.   *90*

[GUESTS *applaud.*]

KING

Come hither dear, and stand beside your prince.

And Beatrice, come give the maid a kiss.

We welcome Hunni and her kin as ours.

May Scott and she live long in wedded bliss!

Bring forth our finest wine to toast the pair,

Though just a sip for our besotted heir!

GUESTS

[*Laughing*]

Hear, hear! Congratulations to our Crown!

KING

[*Aside to* PRINCE]

I heartily advise you lose that frown.

[*To* ALL]

And now we'll hear again from good Prince Scott.

We hope his brain can loose a lucid thought!   *100*

PRINCE

[*Aside*]

Indeed, we do. I'll give it my best shot:

[*To* ALL]

I truly am the richest man alive,

To be beloved by she whom I adore.

I long to spend long nights in intercourse,

Unearthing secrets never shared before.

I yearn to learn whatever makes her her,

Each hope, each dream—no matter how obscure.

Unthinkingly, I cling to all her words,

47

PRINCE (Continued)

And if I could, I'd capture all her thoughts;

I'd pull them from her mind and box them up $\qquad$ *110*

In sep'rate bundles tied with sailors' knots,

Then open them when we were forced apart,

And hear the things she holds within her heart.

I ache to bow to her, to honor her,

To stand by her in good times and in bad;

And when she dies, my soul will die with her:

Our lives are one; our bond is iron-clad.

My guests, if you could know the love I feel,

You'd not believe that yours was ever real!

KING

My God! My son! We're stricken by your speech. $\qquad$ *120*

You need not wait six months to wed your peach!

A week! A day! The least time that it takes

To plan the rite—but soon—for both your sakes.

[GUESTS *applaud.*]

HUNNICUTT
[*To* KING]

My lord, it pleases me to be your pick.

And I would gladly wed your love-struck son,

If I believed he spoke his words of me;

But Majesty, I know I'm not the one.

KING

[*To* HUNNICUTT]

I'm certain you're the maid Scott meant to choose.

His slip of tongue was caused by blight of booze.

HUNNICUTT

[*To* KING]

I do not wish to contradict you, Sire,   *130*

But Scott's impassioned speech was never slurred.

I think he's driven by a different fire—

PRINCE

[*To* KING]

—She's right, my lord. I'm not impaired. You erred.

HUNNICUTT

I think it best we take our leave. Come, sis.

Farewell, King John . . . Prince Scott . . . Queen Beatrice.

[*Exeunt* HUNNICUTT *and* WINNICOTT.

QUEEN

Our friends, it's not uncommon to false start,

Especially in matters of the heart.

Scott thought he knew the woman he would wive,

But now he wants some time to think on it.

Our gift can be redeemed at any time;   *140*

We'll let you know when things are definite.

[*Exit* PRINCE, *unnoticed by* QUEEN.

QUEEN

For now, the night's still budding with bright stars,

Please stay and watch the evening reach full bloom.

There's food and drink and music to enjoy.

Partake; let's let the gaiety resume!

KING

[*Aside to* QUEEN]

Good queen, you saved the night when I could not.

You spoke fine words while I stood by distraught.

QUEEN

[*Aside to* KING]

But what to do with our misguided Scott?

KING

[*Aside to* QUEEN]

I'd like to give his butt a healthy swat.

QUEEN

[*Amused, aside to* KING]

That never worked when he was but a tot,   *150*

But we could bind him to a wormy cot.

KING

[*Aside to* QUEEN]

Too late. He bolted out 'hind Winnicott.   *152*

[*Curtain drops.*

SCENE 4

Castle Great Hall.

Enter KING *and* QUEEN.

QUEEN

I thought for sure that Scott would reappear
This morn to be on hand for Plain Jane's case.

KING

I see why he would want to disappear:
His party parting left him in disgrace.

QUEEN

You're certain that he didn't go see Jane?

KING

If ever I were sure of any deed.

QUEEN

You're not upset that he has run away?

KING

Of course I am—he took my finest steed—
And no, my sentiments are not misplaced.
His choice implies he's going far or fast: *10*
If he cared not of distance nor of haste,
He would have run with Pride instead of Blast.
Scott has a plan. He's not impetuous.
'Til it plays out, he won't return to us.

[Bell tolls.]

KING

The signal's rung; it's time to open court.

Will you remain and sit beside my side?

QUEEN

If that's your wish, I'll lend you my support,

Though I feel ill and quite preoccupied.

KING

I'm thankful you are such a faithful bride.

[Exeunt.

Enter TRUMPETERS, HERALD, PROSECUTOR, JANETTE, JAILER, JAILER'S WIFE *and* FAMILY, GUARDS, LORDS, LADIES, *and* CITIZENS.

[Trumpet flourish.]

HERALD

All rise and pay due homage to King John.   *20*

[GALLERY stands.]

Enter KING; *stands in front of his throne, facing the gallery.*

GALLERY

Hail to John, our just and able sovereign!

Enter QUEEN; *stands in front of her throne, facing the gallery.*

HERALD

And pay due homage to Queen Beatrice.

GALLERY

Hail to our queen! We're honored by her presence.

KING

We thank you fellow citizens. Please sit.

[*All but* PROSECUTOR, HERALDS, *and* GUARDS *sit.*]

KING

We've much to do, so let's get to it.

High prosecutor, call the first accused.

PROSECUTOR

Guard, bring the whore before their majesties.

KING

Ah . . . Jane. It hardly seems two weeks have passed.

Perhaps for you, the fortnight flew less fast?

JANETTE

I cannot know how fast time flew for you,   *30*

So how can I compare its speed for me?

But I suspect it was the same for both,

Else we'd not be here simultan'ously.

[KING *laughs with* GALLERY.]

53

KING

You still possess your wit and agile tongue—
Impressive, Jane, for someone who's so young.
But now we must become more serious:
High prosecutor, state her case for us.

PROSECUTOR

You may recall, Prince Scott sent Jane to jail
To give her time to think on what's at stake.
She's been convicted of a whoring crime;   *40*
The court must now decide whose life to take.

KING

What say you Jane? Will you reveal the rake
Who left you in this tragic, sinful state?
Or will you choose to let your baby die,
For that's Scott's ruling, if you won't reply.

JANETTE

Where *is* Prince Scott? I want to hear from him,
Since he's the one who's charged to make the choice.

KING

He had some urgent business to attend;
Thus, sent regrets and proxied me his voice,
Though you should know as justice of this court,   *50*
I hold the power of veto or support.

What say you Jane? Will you reveal the rake?

JANETTE

I will not, Sire, for he can't marry me,

And gelding him would be a grave mistake.

Such punishment would be a travesty.

I've too much love for him and you and State.

Enter PRINCE, *disheveled and unnoticed.*

JANETTE

So sentence me! You have no cause to—

JANETTE & PRINCE

Wait!

KING

[*Rising*]

How now!

PRINCE

[*Bowing*]

Forgive me, Sire, for being late.

[*Trumpet flourish.*]

HERALD

All rise and pay due homage to Prince Scott.

GALLERY

[*Rising*]

All hail—

PRINCE

Desist! I'd rather that you not: *60*

I'm not deserving of your love or praise.

I'm here to try—please sit—to make things right.

I've ridden hard to Kirklandom and back

And bring good news to Jane re her sad plight.

PROSECUTOR

Your Majesty, you've all the facts you need.

Beg Scott sit down, and let the case proceed.

QUEEN

Your Majesty, you asked me to sit by,

And now I'd ask that I might intercede:

I'd like to know what news affects Jane's cause.

By hearing Scott, the case will still proceed.   *70*

KING

If Scott has news that changes Plain Jane's case,

It serves us all to listen to his say;

We must agree with good Queen Beatrice.

Scott, tell your tale; you have the court's okay.

PRINCE

I left my fête to speak to Hunnicutt,

Who, I fast found, is quite the warm, sweet peach.

The princess volunteered to help me out

By penning lines in which she would beseech

Her sire to grant an audience to me.

And that she did; and I, with great dispatch   *80*

Rode fast and far and spoke with old King Kirk.

PRINCE (Continued)

He keenly listened to Jane's circumstance,

Then went to jail and duly set to work:

He chose twelve convicts he would gladly trade

And offered all—he does not favor which—

"Just choose," said he, "for all are whores or cheats."

Thus, per your writ, he's set to make a switch!

KING

We know you meant well when you sought King Kirk,

And so did he to offer an exchange,

Thus, we regret your desperate plan won't work,   *90*

But there are rules that even kings can't change.

We wrote the writ to ease your deep concern

That death's too harsh and permanent a fate,

But what we have no means to overturn

Is what we chose as the effective date.

Six months is what the fine print specifies

To guarantee we make no personal gain.

It's standard wording, but we sympathize,

Since that's too long to benefit Plain Jane.

Come, son, and take your seat beside the throne.   *100*

It's time to show the court that you're full grown.

PRINCE

You mean it's time to choose twixt mum and child,

But you will see that I am reconciled

To showing that I truly am a man

By doing each and every thing I can

To save both woman and her unborn tot.

Behold the rake you seek. He's I, Prince Scott!

[GALLERY *gasps.*]

JANETTE

Your Majesty, Prince Scott is not the rake!

PRINCE

Be quiet, Jane.

[*To* KING]

I stand by what I spake.

KING

[*To* PRINCE]

You've always had a warm and tender heart;   *110*

I understand you find it hard to kill,

But lying to protect a wretched whore

Suggests that you are feeble, dim, or ill.

You look a mess. You're tired and overwrought.

We asked too much. We loose the hook, Prince Scott.

And so *we'll* name the one to sacrifice.

Now hie to bed—

PRINCE

Oh wry, unfit advice!

It's bed that's gotten me into this plight.

Returning there will not turn wrongs to right.

I am not lying. Jane's with child by me!   *120*

KING

I've heard enough of this insanity!

Not even Jane supports your fantasy.

You can't expect the court to buy your tale.

KING (Continued)

Another lie, and off you'll go to jail!

[GALLERY *gasps.*]

PRINCE

I swore to do whatever's in my power

To save the lives of mum and baby, too!

You taught me I should always keep my word.

I'm doing that—and beg the same from you.

You've promised me the right to choose my wife.

I choose Janette to save a tiny life!   *130*

KING

Of course the king shall always keep his word,

But what you pose is utterly absurd!

You choose Janette because you cannot bear

To choose between the whore and her poor heir.

You're strong of will and loyal to the bone,

But it takes more to sit upon the throne:

The king's the keeper of the laws of land!

He cannot weigh which ones to countermand.

He must enforce each one o'er his own views

And not allow his heart nor gut to choose   *140*

The outcome of a person's earthly life.

Our laws are clear: Jane cannot be your wife.

We know you know a prince must wed within

His class, or else he can't be sovereign!

PRINCE

Then I renounce the throne!

[GALLERY *gasps.*]

KING

Then we disown—

QUEEN

[*Aside to* KING]

Hold, John! If ever you have loved your son,
Say not another word. Your will is done
Without regard to if it's wise or not.
Do not in haste or anger sever Scott!

KING

[*Aside to* QUEEN]

It's not your place to tell us what to do!   *150*
For twenty years, you've silently observed,
But now you act like you should hold the staff—
Your disrespect is sorely undeserved.

QUEEN

[*Aside to* KING]

Forgive me, but no mother can sit by
And watch her child fall prey to death or woe.
She'd gladly trade her life to save her young,
So strong's their bond from blood in utero.
So you're insulted that I counseled you!
Have you no bond to champion Prince Scott?
Be thankful that your wife has neutralized   *160*
The misery your ruling might have brought.
And now I've burning business that can't wait.
Excuse me while I go regurgitate.

[*Exit* QUEEN.

KING

[*To* JANETTE]

Janette, we sentence you to hang to death.

[PRINCE *gasps.*]

KING

[*To* JANETTE]

May God have mercy on your sinful soul.

JANETTE

[*To* KING]

I thank you, Sire, but you could save your breath—
Receiving God's good grace is not my goal;
Plus, you may need His mercy for yourself
When your time comes to knock upon God's gate,
Else you may lumber in the fires of hell,   *170*
While I fetch wood fore'er to clinch your fate.

[KING *laughs.*]

KING

Guard, take the prisoner back to her same cell,
Where she'll remain until her child is born.
No visitors will be permitted her,
Except a midwife, priest, and us. We warn
That anyone who violates this rule
Will hang with her upon her babe's first morn.

PRINCE

God no! I'm sorry, Jane! I beg you sire—

[*Exeunt* GUARD *and* JANETTE.

KING

[*To* PRINCE]

And as for you, it is our deep desire

That you remain inside the castle walls   *180*

Where you can rest and meditate all day

Until the time when royal duty calls.

Then you'll officiate at Jane's demise

To demonstrate you love and recognize

The fair and righteous laws of Cambria,

Your heritage, your faith, et cetera.

Prince Scott, we're done. Go now, you are excused.

[PRINCE *begins to leave.*]

KING

High prosecutor, call the next accused.

[PROSECUTOR *stands.*]

PROSECUTOR

I call James Orth. Guard, send the prisoner forth.

[JAILER *comes forward.*]

PROSECUTOR

This man, a royal jailer, is accused   *190*

PROSECUTOR (Continued)

Of twice ignoring orders from the Crown.

He blew his chance to show obedience,

Took bribes, and gave the prisoners eiderdown!

KING

We are familiar with the jailer's case.

[*To* JAILER]

What explanations do you care to cite?

The stresses of the job took o'er your mind?

You couldn't judge between what's wrong and right?

JAILER

I offer no defense, Your Majesty.

I erred and beg forgiveness from the court.

I ask that you consider leniency,   *200*

Since I've a wife and family to support.

[FAMILY *stands.*]

PRINCE

[*Aside*]

Again this day another shields my name.

I can't stand by and watch him bear my blame.

[*To* ALL]

Your Majesty, I've evidence to share!

I know the circumstance regarding Orth,

And his alleged crimes, for I was there!

KING

Good God! Are you still here? Then you shall hear

63

KING (Continued)

That Orth is guilty of high treachery,

And for his crimes, he'll pay his debt with life.

[FAMILY *gasps.*]

PRINCE

Show mercy, Sire! His crimes are tied to me.   *210*

JAILER

But what will come of my poor kids and wife?

KING

Perhaps an idealistic prince will come,

Renounce the throne, and marry the young wench.

If not, they'll live—or die—in shantytown

Among the dogs and filth and putrid stench.

[FAMILY *gasps.*]

KING

Guards, take the prisoner back to his same pen,

And in the morning, string him up at ten.

[FAMILY *moans.*]

KING

And escort Scott up to the tower's cell

Where he can rest until he's feeling well.

[GUARDS *start to comply.*]

PRINCE

Fret not, good Orth, I'll subsidize your kin!   *220*

KING

Guard, gag Scott's mouth if he speaks out again.

[*Exeunt* GUARDS, PRINCE, *and* JAILER.

KING

High prosecutor, call the next accused.

PROSECUTOR

There are no more.

KING

Then everyone's excused.   *223*

[*Curtain drops.*

ACT III

SCENE 1

Soothsayer's lair; SOOTH. *stirring caldron.*

[*Knock.*]

[SOOTH. *opens door.*]

Enter KING.

SOOTH.

Ha-ha! I knew you'd slink your way to me.

[SOOTH. *closes door.*]

KING

Is that the way you greet your country's king?

SOOTH.

Still stuck on rituals of formality?
Then, let me bow and kiss your signet ring.

KING

If you'd prefer to kiss a different place,
We'll gladly bend and offer you a cheek.

SOOTH.

I take it, then, you haven't brought the coins
Of which yourself and Beatrice did speak?

KING

You say you see, but if you saw, you'd know

That we know Beatrice has paid you well.   *10*

Her steadfast faith in magic arts—and you—

Will pave her path past God and down to hell.

We want you to refrain from seeing her;

You fill her head with dumbing, damning thoughts,

And she, in turn, leaks fuel to feed your "signs,"

Which then play out in self-fulfilling plots.

SOOTH.

You grumble, yet your wife is large with child,

And we both know you need another heir,

Since Scott's not fit to rule a shelf of toys—

I've learned his face displays a vacant stare.   *20*

I've seen him rocking night and day and night

And you kowtowed in deep but pointless prayer.

You think that he will somehow be all right,

But he is lost to you. Beware . . . beware . . .

A mist of darkness shrouds your monarchy.

The babe's your hope for—

KING

               That's insanity!

As soon as Jane is hanged, the prince will heal.

Within a year, he'll marry Hunnicutt.

She'll bear his babes and thus assure our line.

That which you've "seen" is merely scuttlebutt.   *30*

SOOTH.

You disavow that seeing is a skill,

SOOTH. (Continued)

And yet you pose a vision of your own.

The future you suggest is but your will;

It has no relevance to the foreknown.

KING

What knowledge of the future do you claim

That contradicts the future that *we'd* make?

SOOTH.

That you'd ask now is quite the ill-timed shame.

Before, I could have thwarted your mistake:

The princess Hunnicutt is dry of womb.

She cannot bear the babes you want from Scott.　　　　　*40*

If you'd inquired, I would have paired the groom

With someone fruitful, such as Winnicott.

KING

Alas, we never thought to think of that,

But if we had, we'd have no way to know:

A midwife's check can only tell so much;

Yea, ofttimes time's the bearer of that blow.

But we can renegotiate with Kirk:

It matters not to him which daughter weds.

A union with young Winni yet would work—

SOOTH.

[*Gently*]

The fabric of Scott's future's worn to threads.　　　　　*50*

There's nothing you can do to patch the quilt.

You see, once frayed, it cannot be rebuilt.

SOOTH. (Continued)

The details of our lives aren't prearranged,

But some events, once triggered, can't be changed.

Your wishing something's so won't shift the stars,

Nor can it oust the gloom—nor heal Scott's scars.

KING

Then, what are we to do since all is set?

SOOTH.

Forget . . . Forget that Scott was ever born.

A new child comes to carry forth your name.

He comes so soon, you'll not have time to mourn.   *60*

[*Knock.*]

KING

How now! The king cannot be seen with you.

[SOOTH. *moves toward door.*]

SOOTH.

I come anon!

[*To* KING]

Indeed he can't. Be gone!

A second exit's through that curtained door.

I'll keep your visit secret, Majesty,

But mark my words, my visions do come true.

Your faith is not required—just wait and see.

KING

We thank you for your aid and honesty—

[KING *gives her coins and continues to hold her hand.*]

KING

And change our mind: you may see Beatrice.

SOOTH.

I see her whether she comes here or not.

KING

We'd wager that you never presaged this.   *70*

[KING *kisses her hand.*]

[*Exit* KING.

[SOOTH. *opens door.*]

SOOTH.

Good Beatrice! Come in.

Enter QUEEN.

[SOOTH. *closes door.*]

SOOTH.

How goes our plan?

QUEEN

I can't go through with it. My husband knows!

SOOTH.

You're sure, or shall I check my crystal ball?

QUEEN

Well, confirmation's prudent, I suppose.

[QUEEN *gives* SOOTH. *coins. Both sit;* SOOTH. *looks into ball.*]

SOOTH.

Great spirits of the past and yet to be,

I summon you. Awake and fly to me

Through time, as mortal lives and rivers flow,

In time to show me what I need to know . . .

I see King John . . . Our country's dressed in black . . .

Dark clouds shroud Cambria in gloomy death . . .   *80*

John weeps . . . Hold, now he smiles and lifts a babe,

He speaks, but I can't catch his muted breath.

The child's above his head for all to see.

John honors him; he welcomes him as his.

There's no suggestion that John knows you sinned . . .

Alas, the vision's gone; that's all there is.

QUEEN

I see the way John looks at me with doubt!

He knows my belly's bulging too far out,

And when this babe comes weeks ahead of time,

Its size and weight will serve to prove my crime!   *90*

71

SOOTH.

Relax! King John will recognize the child,

For even if you're right, he will not fuss.

He craves security that Scott can't give—

Your babe's arrival is fortuitous.

QUEEN

My husband is a stickler for the law.

He'll not consent to hide my glaring sin!

Blue blood must always sit upon the throne!

You don't appreciate the fix I'm in!

SOOTH.

I counseled you to mate with good King John.

You trusted me and heeded my request.   *100*

John cannot prove the child's not of his seed:

A newborn's size is variable at best.

I gave you herbs to slow the baby's growth.

You only *think* your belly looks too full!

Your guilty face is what John's staring at.

You must convince yourself you're not a trull.

Repress the memory of the other man,

Believe the fib that John's your baby's sire,

Behave as though the tot belongs to him,

And if you must, become a world-class liar: *110*

Remind the king of trysts he shared with you,

And when he claims you've made the memories up,

Suggest his mind was muddled from fine wine,

Then wink at him each time he lifts his cup.

I have no cause to interfere with spells:

I tell you I saw John with babe in arms!

72

SOOTH. (Continued)

You have the means to make the scene come true:

Be strong and win him with your courtly charms!

QUEEN

I want to trust that what you've seen is true,

But being as I have so much to lose,   *120*

I need some silphium that I can brew,

In case I can't complete this risky ruse.

[QUEEN *gives* SOOTH. *coins.* SOOTH. *jingles them.*]

SOOTH.

Queen Beatrice, I see that you're distressed,

But on my word, the king will love the sprout!

I'm loath to grant your grave request—but will—

Because your mind is filled with deathless doubt.

[SOOTH. *rises and gets it.*]

SOOTH.

I give you this with faith you'll chuck it out.

[SOOTH. *hands it to* QUEEN.]

QUEEN

I've known you since before Prince Scott was born.

You've always helped me with my ills and woes—

SOOTH.

I'm grateful I could serve the royal house;   *130*

73

SOOTH. (Continued)

I'm pleased to guide you through your personal throes—

[*Clatter sounds from behind curtained door. Both women start.*]

SOOTH.

Hell's bells!

[*Exit* SOOTH. *through curtained door.*

[QUEEN *rises.*]

QUEEN

Who's hiding in your inner room?

[QUEEN *approaches curtain.*]

SOOTH.

[*Offstage*]

Not *who*, but *what*? I found an errant rat!

Re-enter SOOTH, *holding a rat by its tail.*

SOOTH.

Forgive the interruption, Beatrice.

[*To rat*]

You'll not escape again.

[SOOTH. *drops rat in cauldron.*]

SOOTH. (Continued)

So much for that.

Where were we dear? How fares your star-crossed son?

QUEEN

[*Aside, with sarcasm*]

You'd think she'd know the answer from her ball.

My love was right: I've been a simpleton.

I've come to see the seer can't at all.

I've come to say I'm through with witches' cures: *140*

Ne'ermore will I come running at her call.

I thought I strayed just once and got this child,

But verily, I've strayed my whole life long.

Though John may love me still, I am defiled.

The baby mocks my Lord, and this is wrong.

To make amends, this bastard has to go.

I'll square with God, but John must never know.

[*To* SOOTH.]

Before you interrupted I remarked,

"I've known you since before Prince Scott was born.

You've always helped me with my ills and woes,"   *150*

And then I would have said that I am torn.

But now I've had a chance to think out loud,

And I'm resolved to end our friendship here.

I'm certain good King John would say he's proud

And pleased to learn I've given up your ear.

I want to please the king; he is my lord;

I want to please my Lord, he is my King.

Farewell, old friend, I wish the best for you.

75

[QUEEN *hugs* SOOTH.]

SOOTH.

And I for you. Good luck with everything.

[*Exit* QUEEN.

[SOOTH. *looks into ball.*]

SOOTH.

Good luck, indeed! She's fixed her fate this day.   *160*

A bleak wind blows black clouds from far away.

They'll cloak the moon, and dark will shroud our land.

The tragedy at Cambria's at hand!   *163*

[*Curtain drops.*

SCENE 2

King's chamber; a storm rages without.

Enter KING, *solus.*

KING

Five months ago my life was Camelot;

This day, the contents of a chamber pot,

And all because a tender lad named Scott

Could not perform a duty that I'd thought

Was simple. Now Scott's ill and overwrought,

And now I question as an afterthought

If he's my son, or if he was begot

In sin by some immoral argonaut!

I overheard Queen Beatrice confess

That she—My God!—is an adulteress.   *10*

My "heir"—the one blessed by the sorceress—

Does not deserve the privilege of noblesse!

And yet I'm thinking I should acquiesce,

Repress the painful knowledge I possess;

Accept the child as middle-aged success;

Be blind to Beatrice's sinfulness.

Protected by my throne, I never thought

To hearken for the whizzing of her shot.

Too late, I've gleaned she nicked my weakest spot,

By hinting at a twisted underplot: *20*

"Have you no bond to champion Prince Scott?"

What if I've not, and Scott was misbegot?

How long has Bea been coupling Lancelot?

But there's the thing; to me, it matters not—

Scott's been my son since he was just a tot.

I loved him then for all the joy he brought;

I love him now, despite his tommyrot.

If he's not mine by blood, he is by knot—

He's time-tied kin—no less than one begot.

So even if he's not the son I'd thought,   *30*

I praise the Lord that he's the one I got.

If fit, befittingly he'd fill my spot.

This second "heir," the one I know's not mine,

Could also be a gift from the Divine—

KING (Continued)

It's not my place to try to undermine
A budding cosmic plan of God's design;
Perhaps he's time-tied too, with tangled twine?
But what if when I pass—or else resign—
The spawn of Beatrice's valentine
Becomes the source of Cambria's decline?   *40*

As king, I'm keeper of our righteous ways.
Our laws are old; they stem from harsher days,
When chaos reigned and streets were full of strays:
Sick, feral waifs, who instigated frays.
My twice-great grandfather received due praise
For instituting laws to halt the craze.
He ruled in blacks and whites, excluding greys,
Adjudging his sole line be sommeliers—

As if our blood contains some special blend
That makes us stewards born to deftly tend   *50*
The wine called Cambria! I can't pretend
I think that only we can comprehend
The needed skills and knowledge to defend
And keep our country whole and reverend—
But each successive king upon his end
Enthroned a blood son worthy to ascend.

If one had failed, we might be in a stew;
Viz., torn by war, or lacking revenue.
So God, what should I do? *What should I do—*
Put faith in errant stars or trust in you?   *60*
If what the witchy woman said is true,

Then it's too late for Scott—as king, he's through.

But if I lie and let the babe pursue

The throne—and we're found out—'twill fast undo

The trust five kings have built through time and toil.

A king above the law will quickly spoil

The royal reputation earned by moil.

Yea, Bea's affair has placed our lives in coil.

But I forgive my queen and will assoil

Her grievous sin. It can't become a boil,   *70*

Infecting Cambria with pus and oil.

Our blemishes must never soil our soil!

Yes, "Our." I shan't blame this on my Queen Bea,

For once upon a time I went to sea

To see our navy fleet's ability

To stave off raiders with new weaponry

Designed to bolster our security.

The time away was an eternity,

And I was young and missed Bea horribly.

When we took leave, we partied royally,   *80*

Drank too much ale, became disorderly,

And I sustained a bloody injury

Some way in which I have no memory.

I roused inside a foul infirmary,

Aroused by gentle hands caressing me.

The next three weeks, I sinned repeatedly.

I later learned about the pregnancy

And gave the babe respectability.

The bloke I paid to give the wench his name

Soon squandered all the funds and then became   *90*

Intent on getting more—a risky game

That cost the chap his life. It was a shame

His greed decreed I pay or he'd proclaim

My deed. I set out bait for when he came

To bleed me with a deal. He overcame

My turndown, stealing gems—which was my aim—

Then held he was the victim of a frame

And spent his court date trying to defame

The throne. But in the end, he lost his claim

And swung to death without admitting blame.   *100*

Amid the course of his attempt to maim

My reign, he found occasion to exclaim

My daughter's name . . . plain Jane. My babe's the same

As she who's set the prince's heart aflame!

I cannot let my son espouse his sis,

Or meet with her where they can share a kiss,

But my attempt to curb him's gone amiss.

By locking Scott inside a fortalice,

I've worsened him and grieved poor Beatrice.

I want my wife and son to live in bliss   *110*

And having made a full analysis,

I know our hope for normalcy is this:

Jane has to die, despite my pangs of woe.

While she's alive, Prince Scott cannot let go

Of feelings he has nursled and let grow.

He must move on and make his move to know

KING (Continued)

Some other maid who'll set his heart aglow,

And if he can't—the worst scenario—

At least I know that Jane will never show

Herself upon my grounds to claim I owe   *120*

Her recompense or threaten to reveal

My conduct—or my son's . . . And I must deal

With Beatrice . . . Dear Guinevere, I'll steal

You from Sir Lancelot and make you feel

Like you're the queen you are. I'll fain conceal

My knowledge—simply love your child with zeal—

And trust that God will bless my commonweal,

So Cambria, our Camelot, can heal.

[*Knock.*]

[KING *opens door.*]

Enter ATTENDANT 1.

ATTENDANT 1

Good sire, the midwife begs you come at once!

The prisoner Jane will birth within the hour,   *130*

Queen Beatrice is also lab'ring hard,

And Scott's escaped his chambers in the tower.

He's pushed his way into the birthing ward,

And holds a dagger to his heaving breast.

He says he'll wait to see Jane's baby born,

Then kill himself to circumvent arrest.

KING

Oh Lord, I pray no harm will come this day

To Scott or anyone who comes his way!   138

[*Exeunt.*

SCENE 3

Birthing ward; QUEEN *being attended by* MIDWIFE; JANETTE *being attended by*
PRINCE, *grasping a dagger; storm continues.*

[*Knock.*]

[PRINCE *approaches door, brandishing dagger.*]

PRINCE

Away with you! Grave business is at hand.

If you intrude, you'll likely die this day.

KING

[*Offstage*]

Prince Scott, my son, how fare the toiling two?

Please let me in to see that they're okay.

Enter KING, *tentatively.*

[PRINCE *grabs him and presses dagger to* KING'S *neck.*]

PRINCE

Sire, tell your men they cannot enter in.

PRINCE (Continued)

If you do not, I will not let you stay.

[JANETTE groans.]

PRINCE

I have no time to waste on foolishness.

I swear I'll kill you, if they disobey!

KING

[*Toward door*]

Good men, we're safe, unless you venture near.

You'll serve us best at church. Retreat to pray!   *10*

[QUEEN groans. PRINCE releases KING.]

PRINCE

[*To* KING]

Attend my mum and leave me to tend Jane.

[KING *walks toward* QUEEN.]

KING

As you request, but put your knife away.

[PRINCE hesitates.]

KING

Upon my honor, I'll not cross you, son.

No good would come, if we got in a fray.

PRINCE

Agreed, but if you've lied to me, you'll pay.

[PRINCE *walks to* JANETTE *and places dagger on table between the women.*]

[JANETTE *groans.*]

JANETTE

[*Aside to* PRINCE]

My God, I had no inkling of the pain!

PRINCE

[*Aside to* JANETTE]

It won't be long 'til you are done, sweet Jane.

JANETTE

[*Aside to* PRINCE]

The pain of leaving you, I meant, my love.

PRINCE

[*Aside to* JANETTE]

An unfit subject to be thinking of;

Imagine sunny skies and butterflies.   *20*

JANETTE

[*Aside to* PRINCE]

We're lying in the straw with dreamy eyes . . .

I thought I would not see you 'til the morn.

PRINCE

[*Aside to* JANETTE]

I could not miss our baby's being born.

[JANETTE *groans.*]

> JANETTE
>
> [*Aside to* PRINCE]
>
> You *will* be there to watch me swing to death?

> PRINCE
>
> [*Aside to* JANETTE]
>
> I pledge I'll be there 'til your final breath.

> JANETTE
>
> [*Aside to* PRINCE]
>
> You think our child will have a decent home?

> PRINCE
>
> [*Aside to* JANETTE]
>
> A regal castle, lauded in a po'm.

[JANETTE *groans.*]

> JANETTE
>
> [*Aside to* PRINCE]
>
> You seem so calm. I'd heard you'd gone insane.

> PRINCE
>
> [*Aside to* JANETTE]
>
> I *am* insane—I'm mad in love with Jane.

[JANETTE *groans.*]

JANETTE

[*Aside to* PRINCE]

The time has come; I need the midwife now!   *30*

PRINCE

[*To* MIDWIFE]

Yo, Matron! Birth this babe! I don't know how!

[MIDWIFE *delivers* BABY 1 *and hands it to* JANETTE.]

PRINCE

[*To* JANETTE]

You did it Jane! He's beautiful! Now rest.

Here, have some wine to ease you into sleep.

[JANETTE *sips.*]

MIDWIFE

[*To* JANETTE]

You've born an 'ealthy son; You'll 'ang at dawn.

[MIDWIFE *returns to* QUEEN.]

PRINCE

[*Aside to* JANETTE]

Ignore her, Jane. She's but an 'eartless bleep.

[JANETTE *laughs.*]

JANETTE

[*Aside to* PRINCE]

I thank you, Scott, for all you've done for me—

I know the wine is poisoned, and I'm through.

PRINCE

[*Aside to* JANETTE]

I'll stay with you until God takes you home,

Then join you there within a breath or two.

JANETTE

[*Aside to* PRINCE]

Farewell, my prince. I'll love you 'til the end.   *40*

PRINCE

[*Aside to* JANETTE]

Farewell, Plain Jane, my lover and best friend.

[JANETTE *sleeps.*]

[QUEEN *groans.*]

QUEEN

[*Aside to* KING *with* MIDWIFE *listening*]

Dear John, I know there's something wrong inside!

KING

[*Aside to* QUEEN]

You're doing great! Don't fret, my tortured bride.

[*Aside to* MIDWIFE]

Could she be right? What's causing so much pain?

And why was birthing faster for Plain Jane?

[MIDWIFE *examines* QUEEN.]

MIDWIFE

[*Aside to* KING]

I thought by now the babe'd turn—'tis breech—
But since it 'asn't, I should take the tot.
If I don' try, the queen will surely die,
And if I do, she'll also, like as not.

KING

[*Aside to* MIDWIFE]

Allow me time to speak to Beatrice.   50

MIDWIFE

[*Aside to* KING]

Of course, Y'r Majesty, but keep it quick.

KING

[*Aside to* QUEEN]

My queen, you look so beautiful this night.

[QUEEN *groans.*]

QUEEN

[*Aside to* KING]

Good Lord, you're seeing things! I'm drained and sick.

KING

[*Aside to* QUEEN]

And yet, you look the same as when we wed,
With glowing skin and locks down round your head.

88

QUEEN

[*Aside to* KING]

The dreams we had! And now they'll not come true.

I'm sorry, John, I won't be here with you.

KING

[*Aside to* QUEEN]

But I will see you in our babe each day.

I'll tell the child you had to go away

To live with God in heaven 'til we come.   *60*

[QUEEN *groans.*]

MIDWIFE

[To QUEEN]

'Ere, down this brew; 'twill make y'r body numb.

[QUEEN *drinks, then sleeps.*]

MIDWIFE

[*Aside to* KING]

I'll need Scott's knife to open up 'er gut;

The prince discarded most the tools I 'ad.

[MIDWIFE *walks toward table.*]

MIDWIFE

'Tis well I didn' need 'em for the slut.

He might 'ave kilt me 'ad the birth gone bad.

89

PRINCE

[*Aside to* BABY 1]

Your mum has gone and now I leave you, too.

Live long, be strong, and make us proud of you.

[PRINCE *and* MIDWIFE *reach for knife. They struggle, and* PRINCE *takes possession.*]

PRINCE

[*To* KING]

You said you wouldn't cross me, but you did:

You sent the midwife near to take my knife!

KING

[*To* PRINCE]

No, Scott! You're wrong! She needs it for your mum!   70

[PRINCE *stabs her.*]

[MIDWIFE *dies.*

PRINCE

I need it worse.

KING

Please, Scott, don't take your life!

[PRINCE *stabs himself.*]

[*Dies.*

KING

[*Crying over* PRINCE]

Oh, Lord, not Scott! Why couldn't you take me,

The one whose sins have caused this tragedy?

My girl at dawn, my son, and Beatrice—

Dear Bea!

[KING *grabs knife and attends* QUEEN.]

KING

Forgive me, if I butcher this.

[KING *takes and wraps* BABY 2.]

KING

[*To* BABY 2]

Oh sad, sad child, deformed of limb and face,

Undoubtedly, we've fallen from God's grace—

But you're more blessed of the two of us:

Born dead, while I endure His animus.

[BABY 1 *cries*.]

QUEEN

Oh sweet, sweet sound! Please bring the baby round,   *80*

That I might see its face before I die.

KING

[*Aside*]

No man could show his failing wife this form.

[*To* QUEEN]

91

KING (Continued)

Hold on, my dear. I'll bring him by and by.

He's perfect, Bea—just needs his body dried.

[KING *walks with* BABY 2 *to* JANETTE.]

QUEEN

And what of Scott?

KING

He sleeps at Plain Jane's side.

[KING *removes* BABY 1.]

JANETTE

[*Aside to* KING]

Is that you, Scott? Don't take our babe away!

Until the poison's done, I beg he stay.

[KING *replaces* BABY 2 *with* BABY 1.]

KING

[*Aside*]

I thought that Jane was sleeping naturally!

Her brewing death breeds opportunity

To mend the wounds my sins have brought about.

Perhaps God's planned this matter perfectly:

No witnesses alive to counter me . . .

Dear God, please let my shifty plan work out!

[*Aside to* JANETTE]

It's I, your sire. Don't fret, your son's here, too.

90

92

KING (Continued)

But Scott has gone to God to wait for you.

Janette, your son will take his royal seat

Upon my throne when I conclude my reign.

He'll be my son in name and dignity,

And none, but I, will know he's of Plain Jane.

Rest easy now. Just drink some wine and wait.   *100*

It won't be long ere you're at heaven's gate.

[KING *offers wine.*]

JANETTE

[*Aside to* KING]

I'll drink from you but never to you, Sire.

[JANE *drinks.*]

JANETTE

Beneath your robes and crown, you're but a liar.

Prince Scott was honest, pure, upright, and kind.

You wasted him and now you want to blind

All Cambria to your offense. My son

Is yours to raise, but I will haunt your soul

In agonizing ways if you mistreat,

Misuse, abase, or otherwise cause pain

To him for your unrighteous, personal gain!   *110*

[*Dies.*

KING

[*Aside to* BABY 1]

93

Fear not; I'll keep you safe from all she said:

I have no mind to tangle with the dead.

I'll use this chance to change the way I rule;

Your sire was right: our ancient laws are cruel.

Now come, we have an urgent task to do.

[KING *walks with* BABY 1 *to* QUEEN.]

KING

Sweet Beatrice, I've brought our son for you!

Behold his chipmunk cheeks and button nose,

[KING *presents* BABY 1 *to* QUEEN.]

His peach-fuzz hair, his perfect tiny toes.

He's everything a royal prince should be:

He's pink and plump and hale—and truthfully   *120*

Could claim his sire's the proudest man in town.

We thank you, Bea, for buoying the Crown!

QUEEN

Dear John! There's something you must know about—

KING

Hush, Bea. It's time to toll the bells and shout—

[KING *opens balcony doors. Sunlight appears.*]

QUEEN

I must confess—

94

KING

Then pray to God, my dear.

Whate'er you've done need never reach my ear.

[KING *moves baby to doors and displays him.*]

KING

[*To unseen* CITIZENS]

Good citizens, good news! A healthy boy!

[CITIZENS *cheer from without.*]

KING

[*To unseen* CITIZENS]

Instruct the bellman pull to share our joy!

QUEEN

The seer saw the truth—she's not a fraud—

And I'd forsaken her to turn to God!   *130*

KING

[*To* QUEEN]

Believe in Him. *We* made the "truth" transpire.

Fate's not the lord. The seer *is* a liar.

QUEEN

I trust you've knowledge that you haven't said,

And trust we'll meet again, once you are dead.

[*Dies.*

KING

Good citizens, God gave our land an heir;

But sadly, he has traded for a pair:

Both Beatrice and Scott sit at His side—

[CITIZENS *groan from without.*]

[*To unseen* CITIZENS]

Both Beatrice and Scott sit at His side

In heaven, where they'll evermore reside,

Awaiting those of us who bypass hell;   *140*

So, toll the bells for joy but also knell

A mournful dirge for those who've gone ahead.

We'll miss them every day until we're dead . . .

[*Aside*]

And wonder what their life spans would have been,

Had I not killed them with my reckless sin.

Then this concludes the trials provoked by Jane.

Who would have thought one act could bring such pain?   *147*

[*Bells toll.*]

[*Curtain drops.*

EPILOGUE

Enter SOOTHSAYER, *solus.*

SOOTH.

And thus the kings of Cambria live on

Through royal blood secured through baseborn spawn.

The ancient laws that dictate who will reign

Still stand upon the books and will remain,

But those that deal with misborn babes will wane.

When John departs, they'll etch upon his stone,

"The purest king to sit upon our throne."

His grandson-son will rule the country well,

Not knowing that his mum drew John through hell,

Nor stars forebode which babe would reign his spell.   *10*

[SOOTH *laughs.*]

[*Exit.*

Author Bio

Sherrie J. Lyons grew up in Prescott, Arizona, and is a graduate of Arizona State University. She enjoys wordplay, the outdoors, and spending time with family and friends, especially her husband of more than forty years.

Sherrie has written works in a variety of genres. *The Tragedy at Cambria* is her first play. It was originally published in an online journal, the *Oregon Literary Review*. Her first novel, *Luke's Legacy*, was a sci-fi/fantasy story written in the *Star Wars* universe. It was published on a fan-fiction website. She next penned *The Macava,* another sci-fi/fantasy novel. It won third place in an Arizona Authors Association writing contest but has not been published. Additionally, Sherrie has played with poetry. Some of her poems have been printed in journals and books. After a long hiatus, Sherrie wrote a coming-of-age novel, *The Adventures of Miss Becky McCoy*, which tells the story of a teen horse-whisperer in the 1880s. Look for it in early 2023. For more information, visit Sherrie's website at **sherriejlyons.com.**